D0099976

Also by Valeri Gorbachev

Me Too!

A BANK STREET BEST CHILDREN'S BOOK OF THE YEAR

★ "From their adventures in the snow to a warm snuggle in their tiny and huge beds, Bear and Chipmunk are friends that new readers will want to turn to again and again."
—*Kirkus Reviews* (starred review)

★ "Perfect for developing readers. The large, joyful watercolor and ink illustrations are enchanting."
—*School Library Journal* (starred review)

Not Me!

Valeri Gorbachev

Holiday House / New York

"I like the beach," said Bear.
"Not me!" said Chipmunk.

"I like the sun," said Bear.
"Not me!" said Chipmunk.

"It is hot!" said Bear.
"I will dive in."
"Not me!" said Chipmunk.

"I like to swim," said Bear.
"Not me!" said Chipmunk.

“I am not a beach person,”
said Chipmunk.

"Now I will play ball," said Bear.
"Not me!" said Chipmunk.

“I see a cute little fish,”
said Bear.
“Not me!”
said Chipmunk.

BOAT RENTAL

"I hope
we see a big fish,"
said Bear.

“Not me!” said Chipmunk.

"Why did you come?" said Bear.
"I came to be with you,"
said Chipmunk.

"You are a good friend,"
said Bear.
"That's me!" said Chipmunk.

To my grandson Avigdor

I LIKE TO READ is a registered trademark of Holiday House, Inc.

HOLIDAY HOUSE is registered in the U.S. Patent and Trademark Office.
Printed and Bound in November 2015 at Tien Wah Press, Johor Bahru, Johor, Malaysia.
The artwork was created with watercolor and ink.
www.holidayhouse.com
First Edition
1 3 5 7 9 10 8 6 4 2

Library of Congress Cataloging-in-Publication Data
Gorbachev, Valeri, author, illustrator.
Not me! / Valeri Gorbachev. — First edition.
pages cm
Summary: While Bear enjoys a day at the beach, Chipmunk,
who is not a beach person, does not, suffering one mishap after another all in the interests
of spending time with his good friend Bear.
ISBN 978-0-8234-3546-3 (hardcover)
[1. Beaches—Fiction. 2. Friendship—Fiction.
3. Bears—Fiction. 4. Chipmunks—Fiction.] I. Title.
PZ7.G6475No 2016
[E]—dc23
2015019726
ISBN 978-0-8234-3547-0 (paperback)

You will like these too!

Come Back, Ben by Ann Hassett and John Hassett
A *Kirkus Reviews* Best Book

Dinosaurs Don't, Dinosaurs Do by Steve Björkman
A Notable Social Studies Trade Book for Young People
An IRA/CBC Children's Choice

Fish Had a Wish by Michael Garland
A *Kirkus Reviews* Best Book
A Top 25 Children's Books list book

The Fly Flew In by David Catrow
An IRA/CBC Children's Choice
Maryland Blue Crab Young Reader Award Winner

Look! by Ted Lewin
The Correll Book Award for Excellence
in Early Childhood Informational Text

Me Too! by Valeri Gorbachev
A Bank Street Best Children's Book of the Year

Mice on Ice by Rebecca Emberley and Ed Emberley
A Bank Street Best Children's Book of the Year
An IRA/CBC Children's Choice

Pig Has a Plan by Ethan Long
An IRA/CBC Children's Choice

See Me Dig by Paul Meisel
A *Kirkus Reviews* Best Book

See Me Run by Paul Meisel
A Theodor Seuss Geisel Award Honor Book
An ALA Notable Children's Book

You Can Do It! by Betsy Lewin
A Bank Street Best Children's Book of the Year,
Outstanding Merit

See more I Like to Read® books.
Go to www.holidayhouse.com/I-Like-to-Read/